AFTERSIGHT

Rebecca Goodman

SPUYTEN DUYVIL

New York City

Book 3 of *Aftersight* was originally
published in the Western Humanities Review.

ISBN 978-1-941550-23-6

Library of Congress Cataloging-in-Publication Data

Goodman, Rebecca.
  Aftersight / Rebecca Goodman.
    pages ; cm
  ISBN 978-1-941550-23-6
  1. Experimental fiction. I. Title.
  PS3607.O589A69 2015
  813'.6--dc23

                              2014034393

Book 1

She went out into the streets looking for poetry. She never spoke again.

She lay beneath the tree until spring.

What she didn't say she wrote down on cinder blocks.

He tried to decipher the meaning of her dreams. Each night he told her, I'll explain it to you in the morning.

She spent each night waiting.

When the fire consumed the woman, she couldn't watch.

The cat tried to hold down the image of the cat but it kept escaping its hold. Even though the image was only an image, she wanted the cat to keep it.

The image of the woman replaced the image of her mother.

When she called her father, the number dialed another number, another father.

At the shrine she dipped her hands in the water. He told her, you need help. I will show you what to do.

The world exists between the meaning of being. Not as smoke as the wash of self between the water that swims above and apart from you. The space of surrounding quarters enhances the nave of time. Each word is meaningless. Not because you want it to be, but because each word is a word and the need to drive beyond the space that swims above you. And beneath you and without you. Only to render the opposite. Only to ask why. When it could have been different. When you felt your body fighting the tide and then you drifted to shore. When you didn't want to be in either place because the place you are and were was driven by a force outside you. The birds don't know the difference. The sparrows are back and when they land and fly and lift off again—you will consider the apparent loss of weight the surrender of the sense of what it means to live.

Fragility rests in the corners of the room.
Entire structures rest on the provision of self.

48 hours and light and smoke. You escort the body not through the space you want to imagine but through the moment when space swallows the wisdom that does not speak. Through the vision of you, your body escorted to the place that exists as the place you don't want to imagine. Space is inconsequential. The body no longer remembers what it means to feel how space feels to wonder how space feels. You cannot take off your watch.

Nothing fails you but your own failures. In the moment.

The first day is more difficult than the next. Or should I say the first day is more difficult than the last. The why of nothing is never an aspect of becoming. There is a cloud that persists in the frequent and fallow prayer. The symptom derails the doctor. Not that he wants to see the truth. But as he does see the truth he will enter the realm of knowing.

In houses like these the corridors don't speak. The speech is meaningless and returns to the time when all thought reverts back to having been. The regret is white and cold and throughout the night the failure to understand how to feel is absent of code. The nothing that is apparent in the birthrite that follows the answer to speak of selfish inhibitions of fragrant rosemary that hovers on the jacket that you wear. Will she notice that. Will she feel that. Will the feeling that no longer surfaces ever come back to that. That is a word that points nowhere. Nowhere is a place we imagine.

The world's largest trees sit beside you as though they were something to understand and contemplate. Your face is cold. Your hair is cold. The feeling of you is next to the feeling of the words you cannot speak. Trees don't grow to die. Death doesn't feel the meaning of trees. The trees don't die because they grow. Growth is a speech act waiting to feel the death that is always and ever there in every moment in every space. The willingness to see beyond the feeling of weight. Through the failure to see. We always saw we could always see and one day that vision failed us.

Grave seeds speak as if the moment has passed and the past is the feeling that speaks without squirrels and crows and the beauty that withers throughout the bells. And the speckled tail arrives in the furrowed ground. Remember walking across the field the gophers tunneled. The spice rack filled with possibility. Each and every moment speaking as if the past would not come to be. The olive tree. The avocado tree. The fig tree the lemon tree the kumquat the limes. Their watcher now gone. The swallowed time now. Broken through. We drive through the fields turned red and gold.

Why do you drink from the river. To forget what you've lost—to forget what you will never have again. Pain and pleasure. Cold and heat.

Having not played the flute for many years, and having nothing to do at the moment, a little lost, she took it down from the shelf where she kept it. She almost couldn't recall having ever played it. So that when she held it in her hands, the object seemed—at once a little foreign—as though someone else—someone from another life had once held it in their hands, turned it over, lifted it to their mouths. For this flute really had nothing to do with her life—not any more—or at least, so she told herself. To hold this flute, she said, is to hold a part of me that no longer exists—and to hold that part is perhaps to hold on to all those parts that fit into the life that existed with it. She put the flute back on the shelf—somewhat in denial of that life she once lived—but why not—why not deny a past that could never come back—never come alive—be felt, be seen— be experienced. Memory—what is memory—how does it fit into experience—so absent of the touch and feel and sense of here and now—so left behind in a maudlin, sentimental wash—there could be no basis in reality.

The memory was like a dream that she wanted to have pierce the sudden space which collapsed around her. The couch, the light, the lamp next to her. The music even seemed faint and deceitful. That music she once loved to hear—her mother's voice—the sound of the piano—the music that played all day—into the evening on the record player—her mother in the house singing with it. And now that silence. The parrots screeching in the yard outside. The window—closed and yet their sound just as near as any sound inside her head. Why was that flute sound so refined—so restrained. Why had she wanted to play those sounds when she was young— when now—the sound of the parrots seemed so much more real—so much more present. The music failed her. And now, in its stead, the sounds that replaced that music—the parrots, the crows, the squirrels, the phoebe—the lawnmower and siren—each sound more real and present than that flute that could no longer be played. She wished she had not taken it down from that shelf—she wished she had left it there—to sit—under a dusty film that would grow thicker. In ten years— maybe twenty—who would discover it. Who would find this flute—think about its sound—think about who once played it. They would have no sense of her—no sense of this moment—no sense of her childhood and her mother singing, the record playing, the sounds that replaced those sounds, leaving her with nothing but the lostness she now felt—no one would feel that—no one could understand this moment—here and now—in this space by the couch, the window—with the one light on—no one could find within themselves the individual experience which could link them to her. That's what she most feared. When she took that flute off the shelf—she didn't know that action would in itself claim the very memory that she now struggled to dismiss.

For four weeks she sat by the window, looking out into the garden. From her line of sight—without moving—there was the avocado tree—now pruned—yet still heavy with fruit. If she turned her head to the left, there were the newly planted citrus trees—the lemon and orange—and the miniature fig tree—that held the last of the fall fruits. From this distance she could see that the figs were still green, but it was too late in the season for them to ripen. If she sat up and looked to the left, she could watch the olive tree with the African Lily that took root in its trunk.

I asked her why she stayed here—by the window— for four weeks—eating, sleeping, watching.

She told me she was waiting for a sign.

She told me that in the first week the mornings were cold and foggy but by early afternoon the sky was bright and blue. Each day she sat there she waited for the finch to come to the window and speak to her.

Did it, I asked.

It flew from plant to plant, landing on the now wilted basil. With its yellow throat, its small wings, fluttering—

Sitting by the window, she counted hours—looking from the clock to the tree—how many days would she remain there—remaining only out of fear she might miss something.

The days came and went, slowly—without movement—or rather that kind of movement that's barely perceptible—but this too was a possibility—that movement as slow as this seemed was a willing participant in the now combined effort to see something together—time she came to see as her ally.

How did the light manage to leave patterns on the window. And why would the parrots arrive in early morning and again just before dusk. The lizards had disappeared, but the squirrels were still present—running down trees across the grass and over the fence.

The next week was colder—there were rains—daily. The black phoebe would come late afternoon, perching on the lattice and on the grape vines that had now lost their leaves.

My brain is full of words and images but nothing seems to click. It's as though each image each word exists in its own realm—its own sphere. Where those words and images do not connect and form a whole but rather circle around each other in a space as incongruous as being. How I want to see those things as whole as coming together—how I want to hear the phoebe in the yard behind me and know that his presence is a sign of completeness—or you, for instance, sitting at the table, drinking coffee, working on your poem. What is the relationship between those two images— what meaning can they give me—how, for instance, do you speak about the night with lights—the trees now brittle—the wall that needs caulking. All these images around me—the books and notebooks—the pictures, the newspapers—all these things that I can touch and feel but don't amount to anything that makes sense. The days follow—one after another—each day filled with the same words and images—though organized differently—in a different order but not necessarily in an order I can understand. So it is with the parrots—I

hear them each morning—the flocks in the oak trees—
filling the branches. I hear them at mid-day—and again
before dusk.

The journey of the king is not a story. I cannot tell stories. I can give impressions. So this story of this journey is really a way to speak about the journey I cannot describe. His journey is the journey that we all take—each day—throughout our lives—yet what remains so remarkable about his journey is that it is his. That it belongs to him—and that each journey though sharing common threads with all those around us—really, in the end—is only about us—only about our joy and grief and individual experience. So that when I talk about his journey—though you may feel as if there are common elements that join you to him—you need to recognize that—for him—the journey is unique—individual—painful and surprising. That when he wakes up in the morning and realizes that this is the journey he's found, he also realizes that it's not the journey he had been expecting. So that now—when he wakes up in the morning—he has no choice but to take the journey he has been given.

Through the passage he knows well he discovers only that he is lost. Each and every object around him is a reminder of how far he has gone into a world he knows nothing about. He has no choice. The journey is the journey that reveals how inconsequential time becomes when faced with the overwhelming and undeniable probability of end. Why begin. Why start out. What is there left to gain. He looks at the picture of a young boy. He asks himself how. How has he arrived here and how is it that the passage he felt he knew so well through the hall to the kitchen has now become a foreign landscape riddled with questions that cannot resolve. Each passage through the house is a sequestering moment of action. Where can he go. How can he go. Why should he. The beginning seems like the surface.

When the rains came, at first they gave relief from the humidity, but then they went on and became an oppression of their own. They weren't sure if everyone felt that way or if the oppression was a unique and centered deity that frequented the space and alignment of their system that all surrounding them had failed to notice—that, only before the rains could they understand the squirrels and the ducks and the other creatures living beside them, but after the rains that never seemed to end did they come to feel the oppression of each and every moment as a length of time to endure such unconquering momentum. Only through these days filled with the unbreakable onward movement did they come to understand the meaning of grief.

You call
I stand in the middle of a field
No words
Where are you

The children knew all of the verbs in the book. What they didn't know was how those verbs pertained to their lives. They would read about other children and other adventures and animals and princes and thieves and all of these characters would act on the verbs the books gave them. But the children at that time didn't understand how they themselves could act on the verbs they were given. For at that time in their lives, they didn't question. They didn't ask why the little girl in the story did the kinds of things she did or why the evil stepmother acted the way she acted. Each action these characters took seemed perfectly plausible as if there could be no other way to act out the parts they were given. How wonderful those days were for those children who read these stories who had these stories read to them. Those days were so absent of sadness or contemplation or the need to understand beyond the limits of understanding. How far these children explored the limits of those verbs in those books seemed centered on their lives absent of these things. When the children went out into the school garden, they picked the sunflower seeds. They played with the rabbits, they lay in the grass—pulling individual blades of grass—watching for ladybugs to land on their shoulders. Those verbs fulfilled their every action. They themselves created the meaning of those verbs in their own way with their own language—so different from the meaning given to them by the original authors.

Despite the cold winds, she went out for a long walk. Down the path she did not know. At first alone and strong and with a sense that there would be no trouble. She didn't realize that her husband was beside her. She felt off balance. He could see that so he took her hand to help as they walked down the street. Behind her others noticed. First one cousin came up behind her. He took her other hand to help so that on one side her cousin stood beside her and on the other side her husband. She laughed. Laughed out of the silliness and joy that came with her own lack of balance. When had she lost that sense. It didn't matter. And behind her came along another cousin. He told her husband: I'll hold her hand for a while. And so she held on to both cousins' hands, her husband beside them—and the four of them continued to walk down the street. Not noticing what was around them, thinking only about how the four of them were holding each other up. Suddenly behind them came two more cousins. They asked the other two cousins if they could now hold her hand. She couldn't help but laugh out loud. All of these family members holding her hand as she walked down the street. How many more would come behind them. They were all on their way to dinner down the street now dark. How many more would show up to guide her to where she had no sense of knowing. Of the distance yet she would have to walk. Her husband was near. He watched her laughing as her cousins escorted her down the street.

It was. How do you break that down into meaning. The pronoun—so vague—so all encompassing. The pronoun a description of almost anything—say, for example, the weather, or the days when we were young. Or those moments when we sat in the vineyard and tasted the anise and thyme that permeated the flavor of the wine. Looking out across the valley we had no sense of the meaning of past. It still seemed possible to enjoy sitting at the table sipping wine, breathing in air fragrant with autumn light. The leaves turned gold and red. It seemed to transcend the space that we wanted and expected to be here in the coming years. The walk in the garden. The birds in the vineyard. It absent of finality in those days before we knew the meaning of was. The past now closed. No possibility of return.

His wife's journey. He cannot know or understand or begin to contemplate. Her journey—so mysterious—so wrought with confusion is a journey he cannot begin to describe—and this is where the journey she takes and the journey he takes become entwined—so incapable of understanding of describing—they exist in parallel worlds—each existing in his mind—his journey—her's—each a journey of turnings through a space divided by light and dark and the inability to see or penetrate either. The journey she takes exists in his mind as a journey that can only be fulfilled by a sign that suggests that what we see will at some point be held in memory. As that memory begins to fade, he questions the sound of her voice calling his name.

Where are you. Where am I calling. From this place distant and blind. The voice I hear in a place I cannot understand. Why have I called you to find the connection that we need which keeps us both together and separate—connected by a fine line that divides us.

That night, after the theater, they walked through the park together. They each had to digest the experience of the play and talk to the other about it. They each had a similar but different reaction. They each were stunned by the sense of immediacy and the sense of intimacy and the sense of futility in what they saw together. Their experience that night they would have to integrate into their daily lives, for that experience now tied them to the night and to each other in a way that would ground their lives in a way they had yet to discover. They each walked together and separate through that park now dark, quiet, alone. It was across the street in her dream that she first imagined this moment. And yet when she woke the next day she had no understanding of what that dream meant. No understanding that from day to day our lives could change so rapidly and we weren't even aware that change was happening. For her, the play no longer existed—what existed now was her sense of the walk and the sense that she could not know where that walk would lead. She felt abandoned. Even with him next to her, she did not feel as though she belonged in this world. Despite the signs that the world existed around her. She believed he felt that too. As they walked together on the dirt path, weaving through flower beds and herb gardens grown wild, she knew only of that which she could not know and the circuitous wanderings of her thoughts that seemed to lead in and out of a reality she could not define. The walk could have been taken by anyone anywhere and she would only be a bystander watching the wordless momentum that pushed the two of them forward. She was not scared. Though it was dark and darkness used to scare her. She could no longer be scared of that darkness. Rather—she needed to go further in to it. Further in to the darkness that she once feared. What would she find there. What would await her. The sense of end was inevitable and so why not push forward in to that end.

The language of birds. Secret sounds. From my voice to yours from your voice to hers. Along pathways marked by silence. She walked into the winter evening following the path through fruit trees, rosemary and sage. Beneath the avocado tree—the moon waxing crescent. A birdcage hung from an upper bough. Speak to me. If only to give me a sign.

The box, which apparently hadn't been opened for a long time, contained random objects—an old watch spring, a deck of playing cards. Taking them out, one by one, she laid them on the table in what she thought of as no particular order or arrangement. From that she could see that the objects contained in the box reflected her feelings which at the moment seemed overwhelmed by a sense of despair. How could these objects contain those feelings when they themselves were absent of life. She picked up each object and tried to sense the life they once held. She saw the trees in the garden moving. The winds had picked up and the sun was bright and it seemed as if the day could not end. And so she had no choice but to put the objects back in the box. She tried to remember the order in which she had taken them out. She didn't want anything to change. She wanted everything to remain in the order they were in. She closed the box. She put the box back on the shelf where she had found it.

It was something about white, the color white, the absence of color and the presence of that absence that so controlled her. The fact that she could not know and that what she could not know now seemed a constant state. Would every day be this way—from beginning—through and into the evening. How that whiteness seemed to weave its way into every thought every conversation—every moment that she spent now absent of the life she once knew—or at least felt she had understood. Perhaps she had been naïve. Naïve as to the feelings that were possible and yet had at the time felt impossible. She woke up every day afraid that her waking was a condition of reality. Had those days that passed really passed. Could she not turn back time; she wanted to believe that if you rethought and reimagined the past that a new reality would be possible. Possibility came to be the action of her thoughts. Moved by this possibility to change what had occurred. She wanted to go into the garden. To walk along the path. To check the fruit trees. To pick the herbs.

The food was not only exquisite, but the meal was planned with color in mind, so the plate looked festive. She wanted to have a meal that would celebrate the life they had lived together. In her dream the room was cleared and a banquet table set. She would have a banquet for her mother. And so the table spanned the length of the room. She planned to serve every dish that her mother had loved. She studied the details of the meal. Looking through books and boxes of recipes. Each dish had to be perfect—had to encapsulate the essence of dining that had always been such an integrated aspect of their life together—so much so that they hadn't even realized it until it was no longer there. She went through the box of recipes that her mother had kept. Reading and rereading each one—noting the changes that each recipe took on throughout the years—adding in ingredients—taking out ingredients. Noting the fine handwriting with the loops and slant that she, herself, could never emulate. She opened boxes of fine china and silver. She found her grandmother's linens and the vase from Germany that her great-grandmother had sent. She wanted to create the meal that she knew her mother would love. She thought about those things that her mother would want—perhaps different from those things she wanted. She decided it should be the meal that her mother would serve. The way she would serve it. So elaborate was the planning that it occupied her thoughts at all moments throughout the day. She would wander through the house looking at things—touching things—trying to find the way to best create the meal that would fulfill the desire that she now came to see as obsession. At night, she could not sleep—invariably looking to that space and time when all things would— at some point—come together in a meaningful understanding of the quest she now undertook. The meal was exquisite, she thought—so full of color—the quality— of life—of the world she could no longer see. As a child she feared that a war would break out and they would have to flee, but that she would carry the china cabinet with her—how or why she never thought to ask. She was too young then to realize that the cabinet which held those objects that they would soon dine on had become a symbol—a symbol for something she could not begin to define.

Rather than dwell on the things that were bothering him, he landed his gaze out the window on the fig tree. Even though it was winter, there were three figs left on the tree. The leaves were gone and the figs—some lost reminder of the late summer and the early fall that seemed now as if it had been a dream. The past almost a fiction that he had not planned on writing. And that writing more of a fiction than any life he had thought he could live. Why, he asked, does it seem now as if for the first time in my life—does it seem that I finally feel that finality. He sat for a long time at the window, gazing at the fig tree—and for the first time in his life he didn't know what to write— as if all he had ever written was empty of that understanding he now felt—so empty of it that it could not possibly carry any truth—and the only truth that it perhaps carried was the innocence of the misunderstanding of life. A flock of starlings landed in the garden in the rain, jumping from branch to branch in the trees before flying off into the next garden. Why had this garden become so important. All life now centered on the activity of those things that lived there—the trees, the birds, the squirrels—those things that had no awareness of what he felt—what he would have to struggle with now—each day—each moment into and onto the next.

When she was a young girl she read fairy tales—fascinated by the body's transformation—from bird to flower—tree to prince. Each transformation a wonder of inexplicable boundaries—how could the world fail to present such remarkable changes—those changes she could see through the layered space of sleep. She read those fairy tales every day from afternoon and late into the evening—lying —in bed, imagining.

The weather grew cold for a while—it changed her behavior. She no longer wanted to go outside to walk through the streets—to sit in the grass and look up at the sky. What she wanted was to know how the weather could change so drastically—from hot to cold and how—in that change—she could respond to only the feeling that the cold brought with it. She thought about death now—at all moments—throughout the day. So that the weather did not so much affect her own body but the body of those who were already dead. She went to the gravesite. The marker had not yet been placed there. It was cold and windy—though the sky was clear. How did the body feel there. She worried it would be cold—incapable of surviving the elements. How could she protect it. The grass had not yet grown across the marked space—the edges of new growth were shown to create an outline or barrier. Would every day be this way. When it would grow warm again would she worry about the body deep in the earth shadowed by olive trees. She was not afraid for her own body—it no longer mattered. What mattered now was that body that was hidden from sight—hidden from sound. Hidden from the strange and quiet meaning of daily life. She bent down to touch the grass. There was a small piece of red cloth. She looked at it. Was this fabric the sign she had been waiting for. She turned it over in her hand. Afraid she should not remove it, she put it back where she found it. On the earth, on the grass.

She met him for a drink at 6:30. He'd been gone for over a month. She'd longed to talk with him face to face. She needed to tell him things that would be true only when she told him. For nothing seemed true anymore—at least that kind of truth that she used to believe existed. As though she were dropped from the sky and landed in some foreign land where the people looked vaguely familiar—the places she used to frequent—the things she used to do—all those things that once comprised her truth were now altered—so that even those people she once spoke to spoke now in a language she could not quite understand. Their words though familiar took on the air of code—of a spoken language that she could hardly hear—breaking into fragments that drifted into a space she could not capture. How strange the world appeared.

What she came to rely on was that past that she tried to remember — conversations — places — restaurants and streets—parks—even the rooms of her house. She didn't want to see the world in its new incarnation—she wanted to see the truth that she believed had once existed. Even if that truth was of a thin somewhat amorphous quality—a quality perhaps as ephemeral as that present seemed foreign. She wanted to hold the same conversations that she once held. Looking at her phone, she would imagine the words she would speak—the words she would hear. She would look at pictures from the past—thinking that—if she could enter the world of that image—hear the sounds of laughter—sit at the table where they gathered to eat together—the herbs and spices and candlelight three-dimensional—she existing in it—with them—as though it were now.

She began to fear that her obsession with the past was preventing her from seeing the present. That the present was now too clouded by the weight of what she could not abandon as truth. How short our time is here. So short that in a lifetime—truth was a continuous shifting of reality—and reality a perception of truth. How could she undertake the daily momentum towards that future so absent of that truth she wanted to return to. She wanted to tell him of these things when they met at 6:30—however, she no longer seemed to possess the words adequate to express her feelings.

For even those words she once relied on no longer conveyed the truth of her feelings. Hackneyed—and absent of knowledge—those words were a feeble sound—broken—altered—hidden. When he walked in the door at 6:30, she did not get up to greet him. There was no need. She knew that—in fact—he would feel the same.

The day after tomorrow she would leave. But how did that leaving change the way she felt right now. Absent of a bearing that could give her some sense of direction some sense of place. Here now and in this moment where she could not seem to stray from the place so connected to who she was rather than who she would become. And that place so much a part of who she feared she would forever be lost in. So that the place became a marker. A force that kept her in place—in lostness so profound that the place now became her identity. What she lost in her stillness she gained in the daily minutiae of living. How could she leave this place. Once she left would she be able to find the sense of direction she once remembered having felt. Perhaps that direction was merely a ghost that flickered like light or wind. Or the crying that she heard outside her window at 4:00 am. Perhaps that direction was as elusive as the feeling of life that now seemed to strip her of any sense of the future which tomorrow seemed to ask. She thought about the light and the ocean and the boardwalk she had walked. The ferris wheel they spoke about as they looked out the window to the pier. When the light changed and the sky became orange. They saw the movement in the day after tomorrow. They saw the sky as a sign of the future. For them, the light signified the presence of time. The time when each one would return to a life they once knew absent of a pain they could not describe.

And why could they not describe it. For the description was bound in a sense of failure. And to go to that place would be acknowledgement. And acknowledgement was the recognition of end. She wanted to look at that sky—and feel beauty. And feel all of those things we are supposed to feel. Walking along the boardwalk with and without a future she had only this space only this time. The day became each day of wonder in the absence of answer and the feeling that each step she walked would be the presence of question. Why had she lived a lifetime without this question—until now—until this time—stranded in a place she could not describe. Was it like this for everyone—

She wanted to feel that it wasn't. That her experience was unique. That her pain was only her pain and that no one in the world had experienced it this way. That experience she had always tried to convey—the essence of her work—was now languishing in the distant, shifting landscape she could not capture. For now, more than ever, what she had once hoped to capture was the ego that pushed her into a language she once felt conveyed experience. Now, as she walked down the street she was stranded—everything she had ever written was an expression of her naïve movement toward this place—that—would leave her in a silence that could only suggest a sense of the end. Bound in this hollow space each movement an act defying her desire to quit. Was there a force outside her—refusing to answer her desire—refusing to claim her—abandoning her—broken from the bearings that held her—

The tomatoes were not as red today as they were yesterday. The resolution of the matter was in the orange of an orange. Today was absent of the feeling of color and so that each matter she looked at whether orange or red took on the light of no-color—or rather color that exists outside the purpose of being. The light was bright in the garden so that to say that the red was not as red or that the orange was less than orange could only be the fault of her vision which seemed now to take on the quality of distance—half there—half here— and never really certain at which moment—in what place. All existed now through the amber liquid that vision takes on in the hope that seeing is the moment of understanding. She wanted to see—badly—and she looked for signs in everything—so that the color of the sky now blue seemed to be a sign that those around her were fine—and yet the tomato that was now less than red that she alone could see seemed to be a sign that she was not. Each day she went to the garden. Followed the path through the fruit trees she no longer cared for. No wonder those colors had diminished. Sight was absent of the meaning of the palm leaf of the branch of the leaves that would return in the spring.

Walking along the path she stooped to pick up a pebble which she turned in her hand as she walked. The pebble was the color of earth. Of Sienna. Was Sienna a color—she couldn't remember. But it reminded her of Sienna. She hadn't thought about that place or that color in quite some time. As she turned the pebble in her hand, feeling the sensation of movement absent of direction, she lost herself on the path—the path lost itself in the grass and she continued to walk deeper into a landscape she did not recognize. The grass gave way to earth and leaves and mulch—the trees grew denser. And as much as she thought about the warmth of Sienna this place she now entered felt cool and damp. She enjoyed that feeling of being in a place so detached from memory. Detached from past—detached from those images that persisted—following her—holding her.

She passed through the trees before entering a grassy clearing. How was it possible that she had arrived here. So distant from where she began. And when she looked at the pebble— full of the color of earth, she couldn't remember where she had found it. She looked at it closely. She remembered the collection of pebbles she had when she was young— that she had kept in a box. Where was that box—would she ever find it.

It was still light and that light reminded her of afternoons she spent with her mother looking out at the garden. She had no sense of time now—but knew from the light that it would soon be dark.

She didn't want to go back. And yet, how could she keep going into a night without any sense of where she was or how she could return. To that place absent of thought. Broken from the future. But connected somehow to all those things of life and death that she didn't want to acknowledge—

return now seemed impossible—

Relinquish the notion that darkness brings sight. Each night promises to bring vision and sound that is absent in daylight. You think the nightworld speaks. He sleeps next to you unaware of your waiting. Time no longer matters.

In the night garden the girl goes to the foot of the tree. The frog swims in moonlight. She buries the branch. The earth dissolves.

She holds the essence in her hand. Her hand no longer carries sight. The path through the night garden carries her. If only she knew.

The white paper reflects the image. The tree replaces the purpose of being. All hope placed on the image of the tree.

What will she say when she returns from her absence. What will she tell you.

Has she forgotten us. Or the bay leaf tree. What distance to travel. Outside the realm. Does no possibility exist. Is that what and how.

It was a few days before spring by the calendar. Yet the annual spring parade made its way through the village led by a man with a great bass drum and two men with trumpets. Along the streets, villagers gathered. The air still cool—the sense of time changing and light changing and the seasons moving despite her longing for the past. The cherry trees had blossomed overnight. The ducks in the small pond outside the village. The young girls wearing light floral dresses and sandals. And everywhere the insistence on the coming days. How remarkable was this presence of change—of the hope for change—gathered and gathering around the musicians—those old men who had led this parade since before she could remember. She was not old—yet now, for the first time, felt that age—that age of change and loss and the inability to see what the coming months would bring. She stood on the balcony of her apartment—watching the parade in its self-contained innocence. How confusing it had all become. Even with the clarity of light.

The graveyard chickens speak. Pecking at the grass along the path—weaving in and among stones. He sees them approach as he sits on the grass speaking to her. He tells her there are chickens and turkeys here. Can you believe it, he says. If only you could see them. If only to tell you where I am.

When he found her sitting at the table, he said, I
thought you were gone.

She said, you visit me at my grave, but I'm not there.

What is within reach.

The image he calls an image of distance, the sound he calls a sound soundless image. The museum he enters as she calls you. Calling him waiting for him to hear her watching him cross the castle bridge. Entering to enter the closeness of self.

The steep castle walls do not deter her. From this height, looking out the window, she will see what she wants him to see. The landscape after rain. The sky clear the rolling hills a miraculous greenness.

The room in the castle rotates. With each rotation a new landscape appears. A desert. A mountain. A nightscape. Clouds but no stars. Each movement reveals a new perspective on place. She wants a return to that first landscape.

Her mother and father wait in the castle. In another room—on the other side. She can see them. She cannot reach them. Locked away. Close yet distant.

He climbs the small hill—outside her window. She wonders how she can see things how those things seem to change with her direction. They are told that each

person who climbs the hill will find a diamond. Pick-
ing something up he holds it in his hand then turns to
walk back down the hill.

When she reaches the base of the hill, she realizes it
is too much to climb. She looks down to find a crystal
on the ground. It is clear transparent, with one green
vein running through it. She holds it—wants to show
it to him. But then puts it back on the ground. She returns to the room in the castle to look out at the landscape. He tells her he wants to return to the museum.
To watch the next performance.

Why do I wait for the sound of your voice. If I cannot hear it can he.

When she turns the page she reads,

You
You be dies
You are dies

She sees the final line yet he wakes her before she
can read it. He's afraid she'll go mad.

He told me he would read what I wrote but he closed
his eyes.

As she swam the motion of swimming displaced the uncertainty of major transitions. Movement as beginning and continuum. Each motion escaping the burden of thought. Thought the enemy of movement. The water the green of darkness. The blue unstable in the underwater world. She swam in the pool in the sea in the river. She held on to the boat tossing in the current. The water world washed through her as she moved continually forward between two worlds divided by dark. How could she continue to swim here in the open expanse with the cove far in the distance and she alone for now and forever. With only the sense of that distance as the absence of parameter. Of distance as the depth of seawater she could not fathom. She could not see. Wading through a soundless world she wanted to hear that voice she so longed to hear. Swimming through the underwater world in hopes that that voice would penetrate the origin of her thoughts.

She wanted to heal the birdsong. What could that mean. The phrase came to her and she accepted it. She had to accept those words—those phrases that came to her. That each morning through the coming months she would hear those birds in the garden those birds that each spring filled her with a sense of longing. That would remind her of summer. Of long days in the park—at the beach. Of eating lunch at the round table with her mother and sister and of practicing baseball with her father in the yard. And the garden—the tomatoes and eggplants—the radishes that grew wild in the grass—the basil the yellow finches pecked at. Long evenings of light with the sound of neighbors laughing in their pool. The sense that the future was as light and transparent as the feeling of fulfillment and opportunity. And the drive to move towards that summer light with the hope that it would remain there. With each day came the desire to repeat each action to relive each action to hold on to each and every moment that revealed the moment of place. Time moved forward and yet she had always wanted that time to remain—to hold on to those long evenings in the garden. To remain there in the grass in the light world of deepening shades of purple. That image that held her throughout the morning into the tired afternoon where she would sleep with a book next to her and dream of incomprehensible meanderings through landscapes at once familiar and strange. Waking to the sound of her mother's footsteps careful not to wake her and yet anxious to spend the afternoon with her sitting with her speaking with her. She didn't know what to think. The birdsong a reminder of the endless days of waiting. Waiting for what. The days seemed endless as endless as the sound of birdsong that was there that was always there that would be there long after the lost memories of the future.

He said he would banish all the mirrors in the kingdom. Beyond the aspect of reflection the image would not reveal itself. How she asked it to. He told her that once the mirrors were gone so would be her refusal to accept the necessity of time. The insistence on the forward movement towards that unreclaimed moment when all time vanished into an ether-like stasis of unreal and incomprehensible vision. Each morning she woke to find that nothing had changed. To find that the inability to recover the past was a futile and empty gesture.

He hid the mirrors. He covered them. He refused to relinquish the code that would allow them to reappear. She kept asking for that memory. The numbers the dates the symbols. Where had he hidden them—those sentences that spoke of recovery. Charged with the energy of subtle frenzy. She searched for them. In every corner in every space. In sleep she dreamt about them. Those frail images—the surface of belief.

Inside the village. The first words that came to him. Walking down the street. Early spring. Birds. Sage. Lemons. Words came to him in fragments. Today. Only today. What could this mean. So often he thought in long elaborate sentences, clauses, repetitions and returns. Today, though, what he saw were isolated images. The old homes. The grass. The cars. The dog's nose. As he walked he tried to bring these images together. To make sense of them. To create a narrative out of those things he passed. The red door. The timber roof. The rose bush. Perhaps not all images could reveal stories. Those surroundings that contained him. A space filled with so much to see—in every moment—to find the forward momentum to compose a fiction he had not yet written. She asked him, what is an image. He could not answer. Suddenly. He had to think about what that meant. What was an image. He struggled to find the words, to express the meaning of the word image. Why. Why now.

She looks for messages everywhere. In drawers. In closets. Beneath trees. What she can't find she invents. The silence of the street. The absence of understanding. The fragrant night. How does she understand the way in which each day becomes the next. The rosemary the kumquat—all those visions that support the idea of life.

When she walked out onto the street she became aware of nothing. Not that awareness should signal change. But she had to ask the question. How many steps could she take—one after another—before she would arrive at that place.

A sadness had taken hold of her. It lasted a long time. When it lifted, of course, she didn't miss it, but she did realize how strong was her force of life. It wasn't a force she understood. And it didn't seem to come to her at all moments. But there were those moments when she laughed. When she ate. When she drank. There were those moments when she went out into the garden and walked along the path and noticed that the herbs had flowered—that the fig tree had come back. That squirrels flew through the air. She noticed it when she sat with young people at a table and spoke to them about their dreams and fears. When their energy to live and experience life to its fullest allowed her to escape the sadness she felt before she spoke to them. With their ability to see past the present and into the future she saw their future and that helped her in those moments to escape the force that kept her from life. She thought about those things that made her sad at almost every moment of every day—except at those times when life made itself available to her. How odd is life. Momentary. Daily. At each second. The past seemed so happy.

Memory was tricky. At times it seemed like nothing had happened but at other times it seemed like her life had been very full. She hadn't realized that until—without warning—all life changed—and with that change came the striking recognition that memory was all that remained. That each event that took place now, in the present, she viewed through the lens of the past. So that when she sat at a table for dinner what she remembered was that table that she had sat at the year before. When she walked through the town what she remembered were those walks she had previously taken. There seemed no part of her life that remained untouched by the past she could not reclaim. Each and every day she woke from a night of little sleep. She looked out the window to the garden. And when she looked out that window she could not separate the image of the fruit tree from the moments when she had stood beneath it with her mother. And together they gathered the fruit that had fallen—that hung on the lower branches. She looked daily at the paper in front of her. What had she left to say. The words she once believed in had now vanished and in their stead the hollow space that she could not replace. So many hours. So many minutes. With no purpose. With no understanding. What she had left was memory. And that memory was all that she could hold on to each and every day. From morning through and on to the dark moments she spent alone each night.

When she drifted off to sleep she dreamt that weeds and wildflowers grew on her face. How difficult it was to remove them. But when she did, she saw that it hadn't been so strange and that in fact no one even seemed to notice them. But when they were gone, she also saw that she was left with small holes—small holes that were reflected on the paper in front of her.

The next morning the sky cleared. The water re-ceding left grey pools we had to cross. We had fled to the other side of the island, leaving behind our belong-ings—clothes, shoes, papers, books.

That morning we knew we had to return. Over the mountain, to the other side.

She couldn't do it—she couldn't begin to travel. And when a water taxi pulled close to shore, we told her she should take it. We helped her to get on board.

I left with the others. When we arrived to the oth-er side—to the other shore, we discovered we had lost contact with her. How could we reach her, where could we find her. We wandered the side of the mountain looking for ways to send messages to her. Why had we left her.

A man found us—a messenger—who had tried to find out where she had gone. The man told us, he didn't know where the boat had gone. What we can be sure of—she got in the boat—the boat pulled away from the shore.

Everything was washed clean, including the sky. All sense of previous life lost. Everything had to be rebuilt. Beginning—without knowing how that building might begin. Each detail discussed and discarded. How could you begin again—reinventing a world with such a fragile notion of what it should become.

The walls of the home broken—washed away—leaving them homeless, without vision of what their new home could be. They tilled the earth. They planted tomatoes. They sat for days—for months—outside—under a fabric canopy—under this newly created sky—watching the tomatoes grow from seed to flower. They spoke about the herb garden they had yet to build. They drew plans and then marks in the soil, trying to recall the cloister they had walked through so many years before. They lost themselves in theories of how those gardens had been built—how those monks had laid stones and bricks and pathways through and between each growth. They knew there had to be a purpose—a way of arranging those plants—in significant patterns in meaningful ways. They envisioned kneeling in the

earth, plucking the herbs, contemplating each leaf—
each scent—how each scent could transform itself into
its own unique magical source of healing.

It has gone on too long. This absence. A breach of eternity a breach of time. Eternity no body of being. Where does that space go. Where will it exist. Your face turned to the side. In my vision the thought of you of your each step of each sound. Broken from the space included in the space. You here and not. Where I see your face. Where I do not.

We were hired to be observers of grief. Without knowing why we were chosen. We hadn't applied for the job. Yet we found ourselves in that position of watching, taking notes. Without adding commentary. We could not analyze behavior—only record it. We had to remain official. Within the group. Separated from the others by a thin wash of space. It was later that we were taken aside. I told our employer it was odd that he hired me. For how could he trust me to work in a way so as to separate myself from the others. After all, I said, I'm one of them. He told me that he had chosen me for exactly that reason.

In the aftermath of the dinner party, they worked together at cleaning up, a project that, for the time being at least, filled a void for her, a void that rang with the voices of people she loved. She heard them as she cleared the table of the crystal of the china—of the mismatched pieces that she once loved to look at. She took each one on its own, slowly and methodically, to the kitchen—leaving them beside the sink. How many dinner parties had they given together—how many more would they give. Not in this place though—not with the same people—those people who were not there—who would never be there again. If only they could be with her at that moment. If only she could hear them speak to her—talk about the night—the food—the wine. Holding the glass in her hand, she imagined what her mother would say about the wine. The character of the fruit of the earth of the way it tasted with the lamb. So much emptiness in the house. So much life. The contradiction of living each day now. With absence and with presence. The duality of her thoughts that at each and every moment consumed the space that she moved through. So that her body and her thought seemed to coexist in different spaces—different planes. The world of her thought almost more real than that landscape that suggested the world of the real. She tried to count the number of worlds that existed within her at each and every moment. How to give breadth to the multiple layers of existence. Illusory and real. How could that be. Was it the world of her imagination. Or was it a world that could actually be felt. How could she describe this experience. How could she name it. This division of the world.

What do you dream of at night. Nothing less than your return. Specifics seem beside the point. The purpose of understanding is always misguided. I sleep with my eyes open. I write with my eyes closed. I think with a glass of cognac. The world no longer holds continuity. Why had I thought it had. The relationship between you and me has now been reduced to thought. Each and every day the mind wanders to and towards the potential to see. Why is sight so elusive. Why do I need to recognize the futility of recognition. All thoughts lead back to zero. The infinity. The hope.

It is all part of one. This divided night. The night divided by this. Always in the late hours. Broken and alive. This. It is not so much the word that I'm afraid of. It's where the word points. Towards. Where the absence is greater than all things green. Where the night creaks toward light and light. Marking the days and months.

My mind is a dream. I rewind it. Each night. I do not know when or how or how far it will go. Time no longer exists. Time—which once existed—no longer exists. Time—which never existed—no longer exists.

There there the parts.

A world no longer visible.

Finite the number. Without consequence. If only to reinforce the sublime/you ask me to consider the opposite.

Each line asks. To surrender accountability. Each word asks. To put forth reason. The suggestion abstract.

Absolute is a form of redemption. There is solace in the former. Quiet the noise outside.

Place now devoid. Presence a communal act.

Carry with it the day. Accident or decision. Frequent the process of delay. Obvious recollections.

Surrender is the moment of truth. Incapable of process. No words support the order. All is price.

Each minute in pieces. Broken down into hours.

I—you—a conundrum. The space we inhabit. The circumference weightless. The properties inexplicable.

Wait for the night. When clarity comes in the form of confusion. When waiting acts as a catalyst for movement. A glass bridge.

Through the night garden.

What is the counting.

Each moment until dark. The question you know as a level of thought. That everything in the here and now. Is a question. And there is no nothing that escapes the number. The days divided/by alternate moments of silence.

When you opened your arms they spoke about breath.

When you forget to count you will heal.

Broken elements waste the village. The façade turns inward. The questions you ask seem unavoidable. Guilt precedes knowledge.

Why are the reminders there at each and every turn. When you take each breath I try to follow.

No words now. Frequent the lesser. Incantations of solitude. The source of all healing forms the barrier. To what.

Arrives as the limits of focus. Of stratospheric motion. Of the moment when you let go of the rope.

You will arrive someplace darker before light. But in the morning you will tell me to go on.

Left in the balance. What is. The answer to all things innocent. From each and every solitude. The garden speaks to you. Not in the way you had hoped. In the way you have been given.

Prefigure night to be the imagination of space. As with all attempts the image allows only what the seer grants. Don't ask for privilege. Warrant bounds of being. The words shallow entries in the diary of contemplation.

Irrevocable presence. Where are you. Finding my
way from the tree to the hand.
Where you exist as space.

Laughter excels at the forefront of mind. Being. Not only the age of eternity. But mindful of the argument against dying.

Write yourself the understanding of place. To equal all things. That you would want that you had had that you will not. This is not an understanding of end.

Negative space acquires the tools of speech. In the
moment when you stand in the grass at mid-day aware
of all that is present in your absence.

Or nothing more. Revealing the possibility of yesterday. Don't absent the night. Tranquility rests in the
aftermath. Words summon the end. What you want
and what you don't want. Be sure. For the summon to
forget regards the ailment as lost.

Frequent the sound of nothing. As a prelude to the rest. Where does it go. This. The voyage in the unknown.

Already near morning. What has been gained what lost. The sense of the word forget. Breach space without illusion—the coming days and moments will arrive with certainty. Already at the juncture of no return. The stanza expects closure. What will the world look like.

This is the world you create. Each image each word. This is what we are faced with, how to keep it how to lose it how to preserve it. Expectations surpass all things blue. Invent and reinvent. Each day/ each hour/ each breath.

Language the exile of laughter. Without reason. Formless. The vision. What you see. What you realize is not. Clarity founds regret where all things promise certainty. Follow you now as sorrow unfolds. Why. In early morning. Does it betray you. Asking is the subject of need. The page that recognizes the vision where your own sight fails. As with all forms. There is no form.

Yes you ask. The following. How will you spend each day. Without the certainty—

Book 2

Where the island resumes the notion of change. all things transmutable, the awareness resides in the coherence of space. at once a limitless entity.

Forge through or forget. forge thought.

Possibility. at each and every synapse the word loses shape. only to recognize the opposite.

Recognition is the word of belief. once and always.

Yesterday.

Even here now. absent of the dove. without the bearings of home. questions arise as to the futility of reason.
speak of what is.

Contemplation voids the night sky. absent of purple.
the wait endures the beginning. of all things unspeak-
able. without warning. the light.

All those nights absent of light. regretful. as each word seems. worlds pass through. the anxiety you speak of is the relationship of the word to the space of all things cruel.

Why you don't want to leave the sound on.

Exhibit a.

gods without the word valley.

Nothing breaks the outermost regions. particular to time and space. the absence lingers. in the years following.

The past is either present or no longer present. a form of betrayal. out of all moments without—the form precedes silence.

Forgetting or becoming. recognize this—release you from the moment.

The month arrives as anxiety. each year. recorded in the book of living.

Each year the man waits for the time when he is allowed to remember.

Another life lives on. in the world of thought.

Your hand passes over the man's body. the month will pass. it will not pass.

She sits next to the pool of water. she does not move.

He tosses the pebbles. one by one. past her.

The train. the hand. the want. where direction fails
the need to begin asserts enigmatic restraint. no lar-
der exists in the failure to understand. want is green
and desire elusive in its pull towards night. where you
hear the water fall deepening and changing. you walk
outside. your feet in damp grass. do not stop there. ever
changing. the movement towards all things real.

What if. you were to lie in the grass at midday. the green greenness surrounding you. the path nonexistent. all movement atonal. the absence of parameter the question.

The cat sat on the fence looking out at something on the street. the woman lay on the grass watching the cat. the man sat at the table reading poetry. the water pooled in the gutter. the clock did not move. for a space of time existence seemed a nervous word loaded with the promise of movement. a man walked down the street leading a chorus of mute travelers. where would he take them—how far—into the ruins of a distant city that spoke once again of belief.

The book of wanting waits by the river. ever there/ in its refined state. language effusive yet quiet. why does he ask me to go there. out of this as always you count the number of steps. avoiding marks in the street.

The only river god asks you for silence.

In this imaginary world there are valleys. those valleys mirror the real. you cannot walk through one without being caught in the other. where is the given you were promised.

Ask for the table wait for it in all its guilded pleasure.
outside overlooking the valley. the grape vines turned,
the harvest too sweet, pleasure recounted in memory.
you is the absence ask for the semblance of goodness.
further from your understanding of why.

What if we could to return to the orchard. we would find the first fruits. would we be so greedy. knowing now.

What that i could write about the rain outside the window and yesterday be in the wet leaves after the rain. when we drove through the night you sped. even when she asked you not to, the laughter in the car increased your desire to remember the turns to anticipate the arrival to think about tomorrow. when we arrive we will sit at the table. you will speak french and everyone will understand you. you will be served your last meal.

We drove through the night walking in the street
spacing time as the arrival to place. wet night the clouds
have broken. the earth is smoke. each step across. when
did you begin to desire.

Open the window. where night feels. you of i. wait for the sky to change. watch as he crosses the road. we are abandoned here. we have abandoned here. you hear the leaves. you feel the smoke. you understand want as place. to remember what is.

Speak not of what is. under the sky that escapes you
render fortune released. if we were to listen.

Outside the nightsounds. you by the fire. what eternity to remember. this is a false sense of place. the deep darkness takes shape. i do not want to leave. you say, i have achieved clarity.

I walk through the morning. through the vineyard.
hand in hand. we carry her. follow the white path. loss
already established. we dip our cups in the oak barrel.
this is what it will become. look at the expression on
her face. when she smiles. the first taste of life.

Walk through the night. listen to the words that
fall by your ears. space implodes. what we didn't know,
what we don't. how many steps down the street. for
sight the action of regret. the nightsky threatens to
leave us, stand out here as long as possible, there are no
cars, we are alone.

The nightsky breaks—the face of longing. how do you endure desire. left behind, you watch each moment with the cautious abandon of sleep. well well into the night next to me.

What the train asks of you. to move beyond abstrac-
tions. the plane overhead. lost in darkness, where to
return. to what movement that secures the option of
beginning. when you dreamt of words.

He says, i have achieved clarity. night night. break
the void. establish limits. throughout. where we are.
without. where i long to return. to think of what is.
what is this room you speak of.

What you can't describe. early morning. quiet. the orchard/the grass. anise and thyme. walking. when do you realize that.

Labor was a fragile cow. the moon pardoned the waking. solitude is the birth. tomorrow. impossible.

Last night no longer exists. or does it. this is what it
is supposed to be. sitting at the table in afternoon light.

What is the & that separates stone from grass here next to you. what separates you from. from what i cannot see or think or believe. from what you fear. the i of you that promised. you would be here in the coming months, the coming years.

Return to the table. the morning market. the field. carry the ring of fire. you will leave from the east. all directions ask. to remember the poem. there are no fraudulent writers.

You approach the vision of nothing with the attempt to write about space. shape the void. beginning with the word of.

When she sits at the table you see her.

Count the years. before. each cup measured. what
you were so careful about. each time i left. if only we
could go there. return. the olive trees. drive through
the moment you try to describe. outside. the pheasants
gathered by the path. touch the window.

Who is the you. come forward. explain to me your goodness/what i am left with. these words. reconciliation the absence of sight. before. the last morning. in your room.

Walk through the worlds. each shop. the streets the antithesis of what you know. always seeking. last night. where. you arrive at the place where she stands/ where existence is material. all thoughts point to a reality. do not wake. write through the permission of belief.

Ask the night. ask the dream. speak of what you can see. when i entered the room she was there. impatience regales. surrender acceptance. document the time and place.

How far have you gone into your mother's dream. the night has brought the consequence of sounds that speaks to the ever and everbecoming. with or without you cannot see what you once believed was sight. each world now. populated with the insistence of movement. where do they go. who is they. grammar denied.

Will it ever end this night. what mystical garden
have you brought me. the language is soft and pure.
speak to the letter. where are those words. what have
they become.

Listen. sky extend him. who is the i of he. the who
of i.

Begin. sleep, he says. even when dreams replace your nights. even when dreams replace you. written agreements in the courtyard. blossom.

How do you leave the space you've walked in.

Carry the voice. through each and every space. walk against. and through. how will you endure the wait. you who is no longer the image of i. speak of what you will commit.

Gesture. becomes solace. under white moonlight.
what do you look at. tell me.

What form of expression/asks. always. where. re-
duce the equation. symmetry reveals the false. there is
no normal. what do the words tell me/

To ask for place as surrender. to believe in place as
here. what house will hold them. as they wander further. into and away from. all things that break the division of time.

Book 3

How you enter the book. one letter at a time. afternoon. light. yes. the redundancy. speak. speak. sit next
to me. open the book. the world stops. outside. want/
vacate the past. only here. next to me. what month.
what day. look at the girl in the book/ arrive at the first
word, where does it begin/ touch the page. listen/

who is the girl. find her. yesterday. on the raft up
the river. you embody a life. you hold your mother, you
agree you will arrive. the wind is not too strong. you
sit next to her.

sit next to me/ late afternoon. the first word. don't
explain. hear. see. open/ the. manifest. allow. certainty
doesn't exist. it begins with the girl. this story. will she/

the afternoon is light. liquid. gold. layered. through
the window. old photographs. numbered, preserved.
glass. green/ orient time as the circumference of measured likeness. the girl. do not abandon the sound. listen. repeat. the book is about language. wait/

cross the excess of anger, follow the milk of sight.
all redundancy is the furrow of calm. do not follow the
excess with night. allow only the sound of parrots.

the afternoon is return. to all things possible. witness the light. the girl. the word. allow the inexhaust-
ible. prevail upon flight. see the green/ feel the velvet.
exist in the moment and hours. look out the window,
no distance between then. ever as the prelude to past.
become.

she carries the light with the understanding of loss.
each morning before her mother wakes. at the foot of
the bed. watching. for tremors of dream/ what will she
say. wandering through the likeness of speech.

when I wake I will dream/ before the night ends.
ever. as the absence. of/

please tell me how to begin. what letter. what word. what page. tell me what to do. night light sky. sleep next to me/

find the book, search for it, in every box, in every cell. where has it gone. the story is the girl/ what does she want. always about desire. look for the box. invent the book. start with the letter/

the afternoon. the beach. before you come to realize thought. ever expanding light. what you watched. the sound now diminished.

the first page begins with the girl. what does she say. follow the language as image. do not explain/ all is experiment. allow. this. sit. next to her. listen.

when you watch your mother float. drifting. she holds the book/ what does she see. the water floats. the light is late afternoon.

return to all things possible/ what you didn't know as possibility. the water as sight.

you return to the water and sand, the vegetable garden. the fence that contains the limitless. how, digging in the garden, you discover the underground passage.

imminent. this. green and fluent. she takes your hand. turns the page. parrots outside/ you will discover the secrets to gems and minerals. to buried bones. the way in which prayer becomes snow. light outside. the world comes in. there is no boundary. space resides in birds. watch.

yesterday. does not exist in this world of becoming. what does the girl do. the story is not complicated, resolution is.

the book asks you. listen. see. through parallel worlds. the girl must learn something. all journeys ask. the afternoon is quiet. the way in which all memory precedes experience. it is already written.

afternoon/ she sits by the window. she holds the book.

shallow earth. an iniquity of self. break through. where does it begin. roll in the grass in late afternoon. your mother lies in the sun.

follow the green. space of ever becoming. deep in the isolation of the yard/

she holds your hand. listen. each sound becomes. without realizing the next. before you realize. follow me.

what must the girl do. why is her story important. she's just a child/

your mother holds the book. drifts to sleep. birds flutter at the window. dreams are birds. listen. watch. speak/ write.

hold my hand, witness becoming.

do not leave the book. stay. read about the girl. how does she experience the ever changing. walk through sand water forest. sit in the garden. pick the berries. through the path that leads. follow the bird. hear the sound. all translates. always arriving.

yesterday your mother. opened the book. she said, sit next to me.

the garden renews itself. frail the word she doesn't explain.

she lies in the garden. reading the book/ join her. sit. hold the book.

what is the story. always elusive. please tell me/ the bookshelf ever becoming. what you can read, what you cannot. wait. wait. invent the rest.

sit at the desk. walk through the books. listen/ anxious the word that does not meet thought. walk through the room. this is not just memory. there are worlds here.

sit next to me. speak to me. answer my questions, return to the book. lie in the sun.

why has the girl lost herself.

keep going. ask the light. witness. sit at the desk. next to you. hold your hand. turn the page, remember the bookshelves lined with light. study the symptoms. the westward movement. the miniature book in the palm of your hand. read the forbidden. there is nothing forbidden. yes, you say, and laugh/

where does she go. down the hallway/

will you find the book.

stay in the room. if only to find.

where is the girl. will you find her. in what season. what light. late afternoon. hidden in the closet. on the desk. beside the armoire. each space you empty. fill the next.

the grass is deep green. you watch your mother. how she turns the page. lost. will she take you there.

listen to the world of miniature. the ladybug crosses your arm/ the cat licks her paw. four crows call out in the neighbor's tree. all leads to the insistence of summer. even this room of ever changing. where light is called into question/

you sit in the grass at midday. the circumference where all is silence. sit in the chair/ beneath the tree. open the book/

remember the girl. turn the page. look at the image. feel the page. what must the girl do.

go back. open the book. take her hand. the first sound. follow her. dream of words. hand cut paper. the story you want to tell. sit at the desk. afternoon light.

what is the form/ watch the girl. what will she do.

write the sand. watch her read. become. the book is

never written/ always written. will she sit next to you. hold your hand. speak each word.

yesterday. walk into the garden/ where will you go. look through. always the question. become/ ever changing. watch for the moment. sit next to her. listen. what will she tell you. wait for the answer. listen for the sound. the moment when she speaks. turns the page. lie in the grass. open the book. begin.

NIGHTGARDEN

Yes, I say.

Orange groves everywhere.

Yes.

Warm balmy nights—nights floating—the air. The blossoms. Floating. Fragrant.

Yes, I say.

Into darkness. Beneath the trees. Quiet. Looking back—the lights inside. Standing in the garden. The night air—fragrant with orange blossoms.

Yes.

Into darkness. Full of green. The sky you dreamt about.

Last night, I say.

Yes, she says.

And your mother and father—

At the table, sitting together. Laughing.

Last night—in my dream.

The train.

Where, I say.

Beneath this tree. Along the path. In the dark greenness.

And the orange blossoms.

Everywhere. Walking through. Immersed in. Where it takes you.

Tell me.

When the night begins. What it allows. What you ask.

Always. As beginning.

Yes, she says.

And forgiveness—

Birds—as the light changes. You watch. Hold my hand. Walk through the night. The orange trees. Everywhere.

Tell me.

How the body transforms. From this to that to all that wills the past to become. How the night laughs with you. In transformation of the body to begin the movement to and towards. What is the reason you give me. You can feel it within you. Even if you deny it. The slow transformation towards earth. Towards all that begins in ending. That lies down on the bed at dusk. To wake to the tree outside the window. All is buried between glass. When you walk out into the garden the birds remind you of all that you believe as truth. Why do you laugh. When you think you understand them. When you feel the shock of your body. The first recognition of becoming.

You ask me to believe. In the ever distance between. The image you seek. And the word as becomes. I ask you to describe.

The night—orange blossoms. This is what you feel. Under the tree your grandmother plants. Yesterday. Where I wait. And ask.
Beneath the tree. To go home.
Where, I ask.